A True Princess of Hawai'i

by Beth Greenway

illustrated by Tammy Yee

Bells rang throughout Hilo. Nani woke up and put on her fancy dress with the red petticoat.

"A princess should always look her best," she said. She shined her shoes and put several pieces of candy in the pocket of her pinafore. Nani wanted to be a princess. She walked daintily to school, careful not to scuff her shoes. The bells were still ringing.

The neighbor boy Keoki ran past her.

"What is happening?" Nani called out.

Keoki slowed down. "No school today. Lava is flowing from the mountain. It is heading for Hilo."

Mauna Loa, the largest volcano in the world, had been bubbling with lava for months, but it had never before come this close. It poured out of a vent on the side of the volcano. Down the rocky slopes it traveled. Once the lava started, there was no way to stop it.

"What can we do?" cried Nani.

"Not to worry, the lava is slow. Princess Luka is coming. She'll ask Pele to stop the lava from destroying our town." And Keoki zoomed away toward the town pier.

Pele was the goddess who lived in the volcano. Her temper determined how far the lava would flow. Princess Luka would know how to appease Pele.

"A true Hawaiian princess!" said Nani. "I must go and greet her." But a hand touched her shoulder and stopped her.

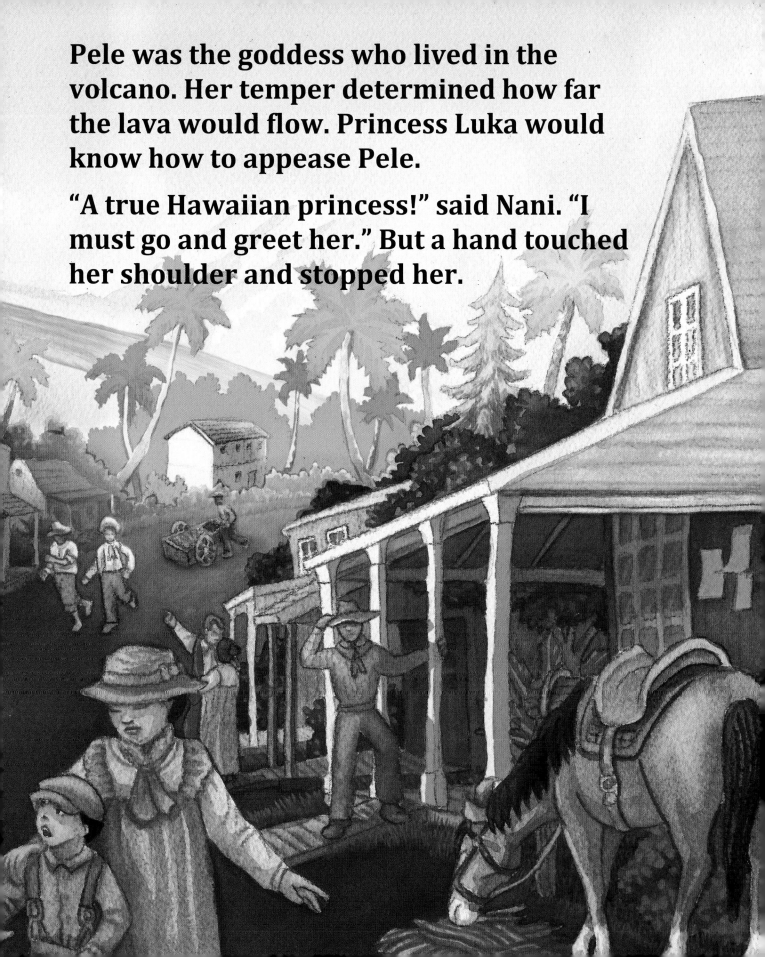

A very old woman wrapped in white stood before Nani. "Little girl, might you spare a bite to eat?"

Poor old grandmother, thought Nani, *she must have come from the mountain. Perhaps lava has destroyed her home.*

"Here, Tutu, this is all I have," said Nani and she placed several pieces of candy in the old woman's hand. "I must go now, the princess is coming."

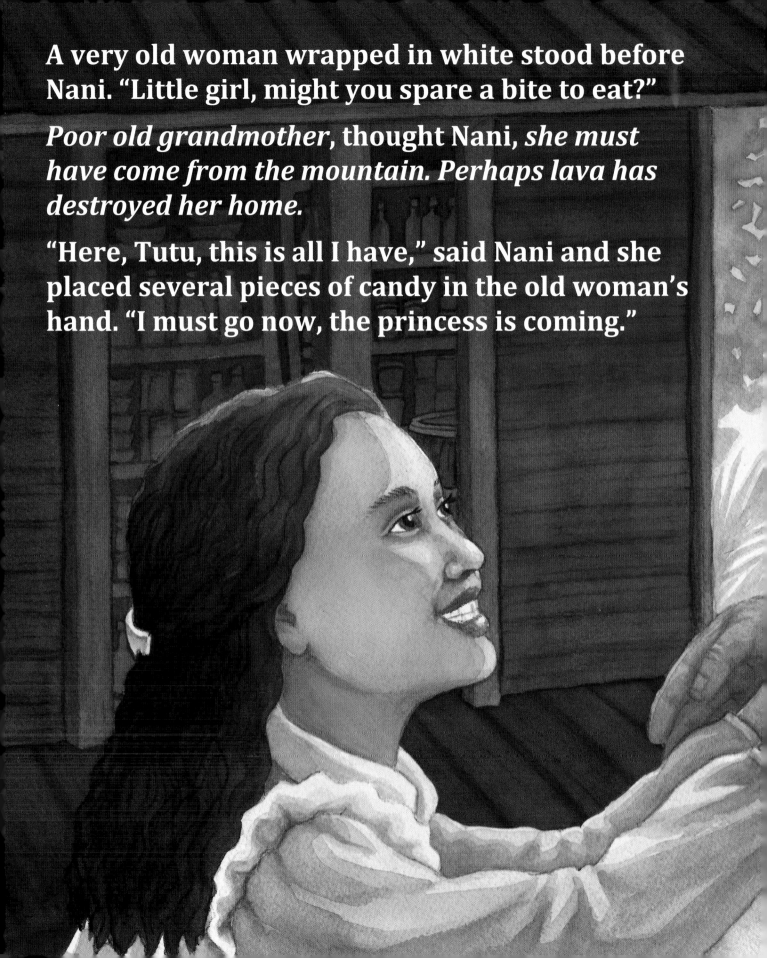

Nani squinted down the street. When she turned back, the old woman had gone. Nani shrugged and hurried on her way.

The sailors rowed ashore to the waiting crowd.

"Did the princess bring her royal carriage?" asked Nani.

"No," said Keoki, "it's just the princess."

Princess Luka, the most royal of royals, was six feet tall. Nani thought the princess looked strong and dignified.

The princess climbed into a borrowed wagon. The horse refused to move.

Nani hurried over to the wagon and pushed. Keoki tugged at the horse. The rest of the townspeople pitched in.

"It's not working," said Keoki, "the horse still won't budge!"

Nani walked up to the horse. Hopefully the princess wouldn't notice how dirty her shoes were. Nani offered the horse her last piece of candy.

The horse perked up her ears and gave a snicker. She slobbered all over Nani's hand, but she also began to move. The horse, the wagon, and the princess headed for the lava flow.

The slopes of Mauna Loa smoldered and burned with Pele's anger. No one knew what caused her anger. Pele would sometimes disguise herself and walk among the people of the island. Someone or something must have offended the goddess and only a high-ranking royal could right the wrong. The black lava with the fiery underbelly crept across the land, directly for Hilo.

Princess Luka ordered the wagon to stop. She slowly climbed out and approached the lava. The princess held out her hand.

"What does the princess want?" asked Nani.

"A red hankie," said Keoki, "she needs a red hankie to appease Pele."

No one had a red hankie.

Nani knew what she had to do. "I have one," she cried out. She ripped a large square out of her fancy petticoat.

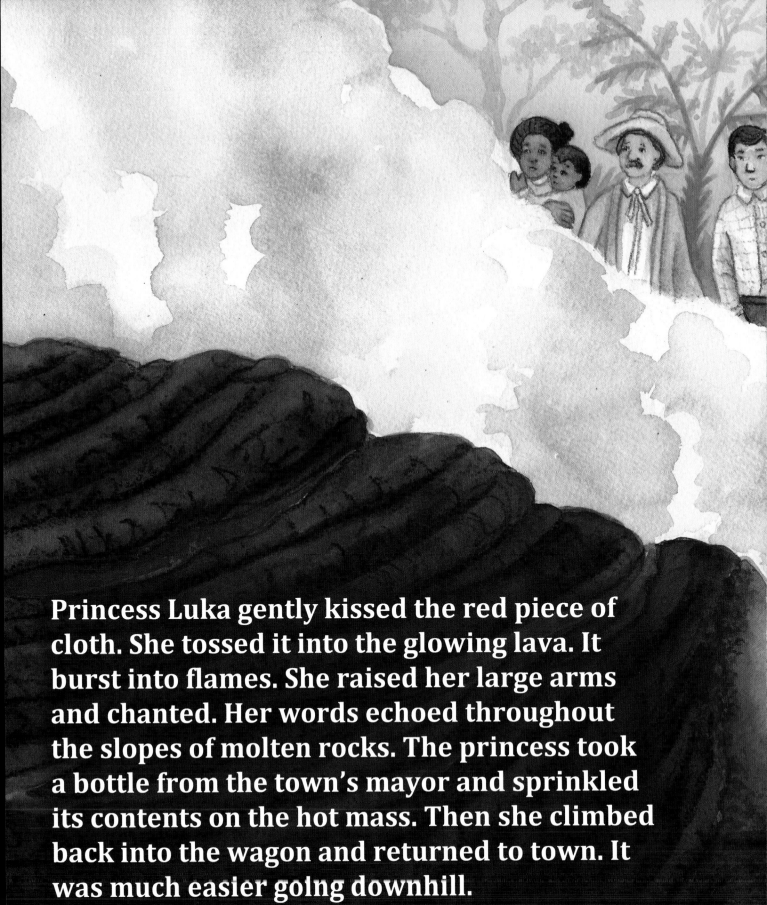

Princess Luka gently kissed the red piece of cloth. She tossed it into the glowing lava. It burst into flames. She raised her large arms and chanted. Her words echoed throughout the slopes of molten rocks. The princess took a bottle from the town's mayor and sprinkled its contents on the hot mass. Then she climbed back into the wagon and returned to town. It was much easier going downhill.

The next morning the town bells rang out once more. The lava had stopped. Princess Luka had calmed Pele's temper. Hilo was safe.

Nani went down to the pier to see the princess off. Nani wore her plain, everyday petticoat and her shoes were all scuffed.

Princess Luka waved goodbye to the grateful crowd. Before she turned away, she popped a small something into her mouth.

"Candy," said Nani out loud.

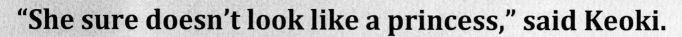

"She sure doesn't look like a princess," said Keoki.

"A true princess is known by her deeds," said a voice from behind. Nani turned and saw a beautiful, young woman. The lady smiled and tiny sparks flew from her eyes.

"Keoki, it must be Pele," Nani nudged her friend. But when Keoki looked, the lady had vanished. Nani felt something in her pocket— there were two large peppermints.

She shared her candy with Keoki. One should always behave like a princess, especially with Pele watching.

For Creative Minds

Pacific Rim of Fire

A volcano is a landform that vents molten rock, or **magma**, up through the earth's surface. **Molten** means that the rock is so hot it turns to liquid. Volcanoes often look like mountains.

The earth's surface is made up of giant plates. These plates are the outer, rigid layer of the earth, just like an orange peel is the outer layer of the fruit.

The **mantle** is the layer underneath the earth's plates. It is made of mostly solid rock. Heat within the Earth's interior melts some of this solid rock to form magma. Magma is less dense than the solid rock, so it rises toward the surface. If it reaches the surface, the molten rock is called **lava**.

Volcanoes are most common on the boundaries between the earth's plates. Volcanoes can also form over **hot spots**, especially hot areas in the earth's mantle. Magma formed at a hot spot can rise through the earth and reach the surface.

Volcanoes form when magma erupts to the surface. Magma is stored in large, underground chambers beneath the earth's surface. Over time, pressure builds inside the magma chamber. Eventually the magma vents upward through the earth's surface in a **volcanic eruption**.

One of the earth's major plates is the Pacific Plate, which lies beneath the Pacific Ocean.

The Hawaiian Islands are near the center of the Pacific Plate. These islands were created by a hot spot that vented magma onto the ocean floor. Over time, enough lava piled up to form islands that rise above sea level.

A chain of islands, like the Hawaiian Islands, is called an archipelago.

Most (75%) of the world's active volcanoes are located around the edges of the Pacific Ocean. This area is called the **Ring of Fire**.

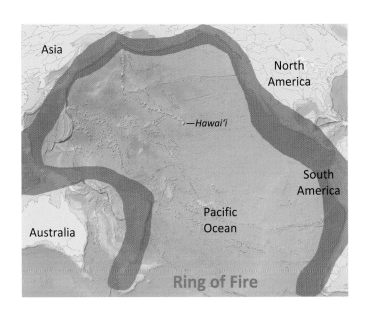

Princess Luka and Mauna Loa

Portrait of Princess Ruth Keelikolani Wearing Ornaments (in All Her Monumentality) 1909

Princess Ruth Luka Keanolani Kauanāhoahoa Keʻelikōlani was born in 1826. She was part of the Kamehameha royal family of the Kingdom of Hawaiʻi. Her mother, High Chiefess Kalani Pauahi, died giving birth to her, and her mother's husband sent the baby princess away. Queen Kaahumanu adopted Princess Luka.

Princess Luka was the Royal Governor of the Island of Hawaiʻi, a major landowner, and the wealthiest woman in the islands. The people of Hawaiʻi loved and respected her.

On November 5, 1880, a volcano called Mauna Loa started to erupt. Over the next few months, thick lava crept toward the town of Hilo. The townspeople could see the glow of forests burning. In June of 1881, the lava was only five miles from Hilo. The town organized a day of prayer. But the lava kept coming. It moved 100-500 feet each day. In late July, Princess Luka travelled to Hilo. A borrowed wagon took her to the lava flow. By August 10, 1881, the flow stopped. It was only a mile and a half away from Hilo Bay. The town was safe.

When Princess Luka died, she left most of her property to her cousin. Princess Bernice Pauahi used Princess Luka's wealth to form schools for the children of Hawaiʻi. To this day, the Kamehameha Schools teach the Hawaiian language and the hula . . . and Princess Luka's love for her people and culture lives on.

Fact or fiction?

The story in this book is fiction, but it is based on a true story (above). Compare the two versions and answer the following questions based on the historical facts.

1. Was Princess Luka a real person or a fictional character?

2. Were Nani and Keoki real people or fictional characters?

3. Did the lava flow from Mauna Loa move fast or slow?

4. How did Princess Luka travel from the shore to the lava flow?

5. Did the lava stop as soon as Princess Luka arrived?

Volcanic Vocabulary Matching

Match the volcano terms with their location on the next page.

ash: tiny pieces of rock and volcanic glass that are exploded or carried into the air during an eruption. Ash can be carried by the wind for great distances from the vent.

conduit: the path magma travels from the magma chamber to the vent. A conduit can have one direct path from the magma chamber to the surface, or it can split and lead to multiple vents.

crust: the solid, top layer of the earth, which forms the continents and the land under the oceans.

lava: molten rock erupted at the surface. Lava cools and hardens as it flows along the ground.

magma chamber: a place within a volcano where magma is stored before an eruption. When pressure builds inside the chamber, magma moves to the surface, where it erupts from a volcanic vent.

mantle: the layer of mostly solid rock underneath the earth's crust.

vent: where magma is erupted on to the earth's surface. On Hawaiian volcanoes, vents often open at the summit (top) and along the flanks (sides) of the volcano.

Respect Hawai'i's Natural Resources!

People who visit Hawai'i should be careful to not interfere with or harm any of Hawai'i's natural resources. This includes flowing lava. Throwing anything into the lava is disrespectful to many Native Hawaiians and, in some areas, it is against the law.

You can share the beauty and wonder of nature with those who come after you! When you visit Hawai'i's volcanoes, or any other natural habitat, respect the environment.

Answers: A-ash. B-vent. C-lava. D-conduit. E-magma chamber. F-crust. G-mantle.

There are five volcanoes on the Island of Hawai'i. Look for the numbers on the map below to identify each of the five volcanoes.

1. Kohala
2. Mauna Kea
3. Hualālai
4. Mauna Loa
5. Kīlauea

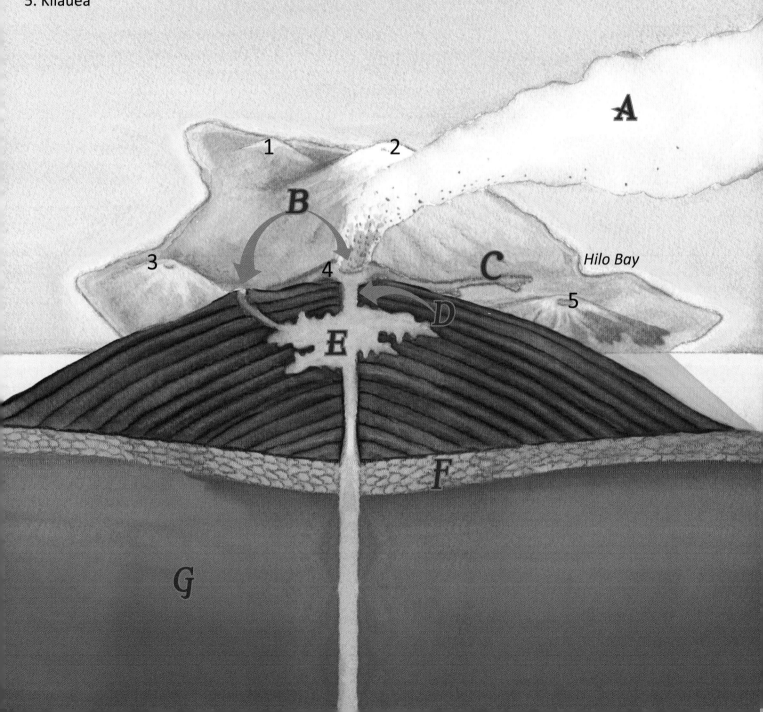

To my three daughters, Kealani, Ka'ipolani and Pua'enalani.—BG

Thanks to Dr. Barbara Moir, President and Curator of Education at the Lyman Museum in Hilo, HI, for verifying the accuracy of the information in this book.

Library of Congress Cataloging-in-Publication Data

Names: Greenway, Beth, author. | Yee, Tammy, illustrator.
Title: A true princess of Hawai'i / by Beth Greenway ; illustrated by Tammy Yee.
Description: Mount Pleasant, SC : Arbordale Publishing, [2017] | Summary: "Nani learns that there is more to being a princess than fine clothes when a real Hawaiian princess comes to save the town of Hilo from Mauna Loa's volcanic lava flow. Based on the historical events of the 1880-1881 eruption of Mauna Loa on the Island of Hawai'i"-- Provided by publisher. | Includes bibliographical references.
Identifiers: LCCN 2016043595 (print) | LCCN 2016048981 (ebook) | ISBN 9781628559484 (english hardcover) | ISBN 9781628559491 (english pbk.) | ISBN 9781628559507 (spanish pbk.) | ISBN 9781628559514 (English Downloadable eBook) | ISBN 9781628559538 (English Interactive Dual-Language eBook) | ISBN 9781628559521 (Spanish Downloadable eBook) | ISBN 9781628559545 (Spanish Interactive Dual-Language eBook)
Subjects: | CYAC: Princesses--Fiction. | Volcanoes--Fiction. | Hawaii--History--To 1893--Fiction.
Classification: LCC PZ7.G8524 Tr 2017 (print) | LCC PZ7.G8524 (ebook) | DDC [E]--dc23
LC record available at https://lccn.loc.gov/2016043595

Translated into Spanish: *Una verdadera Princesa de Hawái*

Lexile® Level: 560L

key phrases: based on a true story, character, earth layers, Hawaii, historical events, map, natural disasters, Pacific, plate tectonics, volcanoes

Bibliography:

Free, David. *Vignettes of Old Hawai'i*. Honolulu: Crossroads Press, Inc., 1994. Print.

Varez, Dietrich and Pua Kanaka'ole Kanahele. *Pele*. Honolulu: Bishop Museum Press, 1991. Print.

Rice, William Hyde. "The Goddess Pele". Pacific Anthropological Record 30 (1980): 123-126. Print.

National Park Service. National Park Hawai'i. 2015. Web.

Williams, Ronald Jr. *Pa ki'i of Princess Ruth Ke'elikolani*. Bishop Museum 2005-2011. Web. 20 March 2015.

Hori, Joan. *Background and Historical Significance of Ka Nu Pepa Kuakoa*. University of Hawai'i, 2001. Web. 20 March 2015.

Manufactured in China, December 2016
This product conforms to CPSIA 2008
First Printing

Arbordale Publishing
Mt. Pleasant, SC 29464
www.ArbordalePublishing.com